W9-ABD-969

# AMAZING TRUE STORIES

# AMAZING TRUE STORIES

Don L. Wulffson
Illustrated by John R. Jones



COBBLEHILL BOOKS
Dutton New York

*For Gwen, a very special young lady*



Library of Congress Cataloging-in-Publication Data
Wulffson, Don L.
Amazing true stories / Don L. Wulffson ; illustrated by John R. Jones.
p. cm.
Summary: A collection of unusual stories that are hard to believe but true, in such categories as "Travel and Transportation," "Crime and Punishment," and "Accidents and Disasters."
ISBN 0-525-65070-9
1. Curiosities and wonders—Juvenile literature. [1. Curiosities and wonders.]
I. Jones, John R., ill. II. Title.
AG243.W83 1991 031—dc20 90-28105 CIP AC

Published in the United States by Cobblehill Books,
an affiliate of Dutton Children's Books,
a division of Penguin USA Inc.

Designed by Jean Krulis
Printed in the United States of America
First Edition 10 9 8 7 6 5 4 3 2 1

# CONTENTS

## TRAVEL AND TRANSPORTATION



## CRIME AND PUNISHMENT

## ACCIDENTS AND DISASTERS



## ART AND LITERATURE



## SCIENCE



## POLITICS AND GOVERNMENT

## THE UNKNOWN AND MYSTERIOUS



## ALL IN SPORT



## WEIRD WEATHER

# Travel and Transportation

# A Package for Grandma

In 1914, May Pierstorff's parents wanted to send their four-year-old daughter to visit her grandmother. But the Pierstorffs were poor. The price of an ordinary train ticket for the 100-mile trip to Lewiston, Idaho, was more than they could possibly afford. After much thinking, the Pierstorffs came up with a very cheap—and very unusual—way to transport their child.

They decided *to mail her* to her grandmother.

At the post office, the postmaster studied all the rules. Little May fit the weight requirements. She weighed 48 pounds; 50 was the limit. It was not legal to send live animals through the mail—except for baby chicks. The postmaster decided she fit the category. He listed her as a 48-pound baby chick! He collected 53 cents in postage from her parents, and glued the stamps to a tag on the little girl's coat.

May was driven to the depot and put into the mail baggage car. On her journey, she was under the care of the train baggageman. Arriving in Lewiston, she was taken to the post office. The custom was to leave packages there overnight. However, a kindly clerk made an exception. He stopped his work and made a special delivery of the little girl to her grandmother.

# A Funny Thing Happened on the Way to . . .

Have you ever felt that some drivers on the road are a bit wacky, a bit confused? Does it look to you like the only place they're headed is into an accident?

Read some actual insurance accident reports. The writers were asked to describe very simply and very clearly what happened. Their writing skills turned out to be about as sharp as their driving skills . . .

The guy was all over the road; I had to swerve a number of times before I hit him.

I had been driving my car for 40 years, when I fell asleep at the wheel and had an accident.

The telephone pole was approaching fast. I was attempting to swerve out of its path when it struck my front end.

I was on my way to the doctor's with rear end trouble when my universal joint gave way causing me to have an accident.

An invisible car came out of nowhere, struck my vehicle, and vanished.

I saw the slow-moving sad-faced old gentleman as he bounced off the hood of my car.

Coming home, I drove into the wrong house and collided with a tree I don't have.

I was unable to stop in time and my car crashed into the other vehicle. The driver and passengers then left immediately for a vacation with injuries.

In my attempt to kill a fly, I drove into a telephone pole.

The pedestrian had no idea which direction to go, so I ran over him.

The indirect cause of this accident was a little guy in a small car with a big mouth.

I thought my window was down, but I found out it was up when I put my hand through it.

My car was legally parked as it backed into the other vehicle.

I was thrown from my car as it left the road. I was later found in a ditch by some stray cows.

# The Man in the Flying Chair

Larry Walters, 33, lived in San Pedro, California. His girl friend lived over a hundred miles away, in a desert town. Larry wanted to go see her.

Nothing unusual about that. What *was* unusual was how Larry planned to get from San Pedro to the desert.

Larry rigged forty-two weather balloons to an aluminum lawn chair. He and a few friends pumped the balloons full of helium. He sat down in the chair. Larry gave a thumbs-up signal.

His friends slowly let out the lines that held the chair. Suddenly, one of the lines broke. The jolt caused the others to lose their grip. Larry shot upward.

"It kind of shocked me when it let go," he said later. "It knocked my glasses off. I couldn't see very well, and I was really going up fast."

In hardly any time at all he was at 16,000 feet. A startled jetliner pilot spotted him. He radioed back that "Some crazy guy just flew past in a chair!"

"That jet plane flashing past scared me," said Larry. "But the view was great. I had a camera along, but I didn't take

any pictures. Not one. I was too amazed by what I was seeing with my own eyes."

Larry had wanted to go all the way to his girl friend's house. But there was almost no wind. He was hardly moving along at all.

"I had gone only about 50 miles," said Larry. "I was over Long Beach. I knew I wasn't going to make it to the desert. But I wasn't even thinking about that anymore. I was getting scared, and it was cold. That was the worst thing. Especially my face and feet. They were freezing."

Ice-cold—and going almost nowhere—Larry had had enough. After almost two hours in the air, his only thoughts were of getting down alive.

"I was prepared," he said. "I had a pellet gun. I started shooting at the balloons. As each one popped, I'd go a little lower. After a while, I was gliding over streets and buildings and houses. That was the scariest part of all. I was sure I was going to crash into something and get killed. I was especially afraid my aluminum chair would hit the power lines, and I'd get electrocuted."

He almost did. In his chair, he floated under some power lines. The balloons caught on the wires, stopping him. He swung back and forth for a few minutes. Then he edged out of his chair—and dropped to the ground.

Safe and sound.

"You ever plan to do this again?" a reporter asked Larry later.

He laughed and shook his head. "It was something else," he said. "I'll never forget it. But it was a stupid thing to try. I'm just lucky to be alive."

# Buddy-system Driving

A few years ago in Jackson, Mississippi, a policeman was on traffic patrol. He noticed a car that was zigzagging wildly through traffic. Flipping on his siren and lights, he went in pursuit. After a short chase, he brought the car to a halt.

Two men were seated in the car.

When the policeman asked the driver for his license, he explained that he had none. "I can't get a license," said the driver as he took off dark glasses. "Fact is, I'm blind," he added, turning his head in the general direction of the policeman.

"Then what in the world are you doing driving a car!" demanded the officer.

The blind man shrugged and pointed toward the man in the seat next to him. "My friend here is giving me directions. But he's plastered. He's way too drunk to drive by himself. He was doin' the seein' and I was doin' the steerin'. Pretty good idea, huh?"

The policeman didn't agree. He arrested both men and took them to jail.

# He Knew There Was Something He'd Forgotten

It happens to all of us. We return home from a vacation. Then we discover we left something behind.

That's what happened to Ken Zimmer. But his case is more unusual than most.

Over the Christmas holiday in 1988, Zimmer took his family on a trip to San Francisco. He and his wife and five children spent a week in the city. When the week was up, they headed for home in the family van. Home was Eugene, Oregon, several hundred miles north of San Francisco.

They drove all night. It was a long, tiring haul.

It was dawn when Zimmer finally pulled into the driveway of his home. That's when it hit him. That's when Zimmer realized he'd left something behind.

His wife!

About halfway home, they had stopped for something to eat. After they had eaten, Ken slid in behind the wheel. The others crawled into the back of the van. Ken headed out onto the highway—and was soon whizzing along. And everybody else was in the back of the van, settling down for a long snooze.

Everybody, that is, except Ken's wife, Pat.

She was running through the parking lot after the departing van. It disappeared into the darkness. She waited, knowing he'd soon realize she wasn't aboard.

He didn't, not until five hours later, as he pulled into his own driveway.

Worried sick, Ken filed a missing persons report with the police.

That afternoon, a call came. It was from his wife. She had taken a bus back to Eugene. She was at the bus station, and needed a lift.

Red-faced but relieved, Ken drove down to get her.

# No Dogs Allowed

Thousands of people cross the Golden Gate Bridge, in and out of San Francisco, every day. To cross it, motorists have to stop at a toll booth and pay $1 or $2, depending on the day of the week. If a person does not have the money, he or she can leave something equal in value to the toll. The item is tagged. Then the owner can return later and pay the toll to get it back.

But sometimes the people don't come back. All sorts of strange items pile up.

Over the years, drivers have left the following items: a can of motor oil, a tool kit, rock 'n' roll cassettes, a set of silver tableware, a TV, men's wedding rings (these are left by the dozens), a set of false teeth, swim fins, a blouse, a frying pan, and a toilet plunger.

The most expensive item ever left was a $7,000 diamond wristwatch. Years passed. The owner still did not pick it up. Finally it was sold at auction for $5.

There are some things the toll officers cannot accept. People have tried to leave such things as uncanned food, their driver's license, even their eyeglasses. The strangest was a man who wanted to leave his dog. The toll booth operator settled for the collar.

# Long-lost Stranger

In 1975, the Williams sisters went to the London airport to meet a long-lost brother. They drove home with a complete stranger.

"There he is!" they shouted as a nice-looking young man got off the plane. The sisters hugged him and smothered him with kisses.

Steve Stone of Buffalo, New York, was surprised. But he was also pleased at all the affection four pretty young women were showing him. "Gee, this is great!" he kept saying.

They hustled him off to their car. They even carried his suitcases for him.

"Are you this nice to everyone?" he said with a wink.

"No, silly, just the ones we love!" said one of the sisters.

"Well, this sure is great!" said Mr. Stone again as they drove off in the car.

"Well, it's great for us, too," said one of the sisters.

"It was such a hard thing," added another. "Us girls in England, and you bein' sent to live in America."

"Huh?" said Stone.

"Heavens, I was only twelve the last time I saw you," said another.

"What?" blurted Stone. "I've never seen any of you before in my life!"

The driver slammed on the brakes. A lot of explaining was done. Embarrassed, they drove back to the airport.

Stone wandered off to find a taxi.

In the lobby of the airport, the girls spotted a lonely looking young man. He was sitting by himself, wondering what had become of his long-lost sisters.

# Crime and Punishment

# Bad Break

In 1959, a man made a daring escape from a prison in Sydney, Australia. However, things did not work out exactly as he had planned.

The prisoner escaped by climbing underneath the hood of a van. The van was delivering bread to the prison.

He squeezed his body over and around the engine, then pulled the hood closed. It was a cramped, dirty, and hot hiding place. Still, the prisoner must have smiled when the van was started up and headed out through the prison gate.

After a short journey, the van came to a stop. Waiting until it sounded as if the coast were clear, the prisoner lifted the hood and crawled out of his dark, greasy hiding place. What he saw couldn't have made him very happy. The van was parked inside the yard of another prison just four miles from the first!

Two guards had already spotted him. Their guns were drawn. "Hold it right there!" yelled one of the guards.

Certainly, there was nowhere to run. The man hung his

head and raised his hands. Then he was taken to a cell.

The next morning the man was returned to his own prison—in a paddy wagon, not a bread truck.

# The Worst Bank Robbers

Down through history, there have been many shrewd, brilliantly planned robberies. This is not the story of one of them.

In August, 1975, three men were on their way to rob a bank in Scotland. On their way into the bank, they got stuck in the revolving doors. People in the bank laughed. A smiling security guard, not knowing what they were up to, came and helped free them. After thanking him, the three robbers sheepishly left the building.

A few minutes later the men decided to try again. This time they were able to make their way into the bank without getting stuck. "OK, this is a bank robbery," said the gang leader nervously.

Everyone in the bank started laughing. Obviously, it was a joke. After all, weren't these the same three silly men who had just gotten stuck in the revolving doors?

The bank robbers were getting mad, and also embarrassed. "What's wrong with ya?" stuttered the leader. "This is for real. And we want ten thousand dollars!"

The head cashier could hardly control herself. She almost fell down laughing.

The robbers weren't getting anywhere. They wondered perhaps if they were asking too much. The gang leader lowered his demand to $1,000, then to $100, then to a dollar each.

At this point, everyone in the bank was howling with laughter.

Angry, one of the robbers pulled out a pistol. Then he jumped up on the counter to get everyone's attention. He stumbled and fell with a crash, breaking his leg.

The other two made their getaway. They pushed their way out through the revolving doors. But the door only went halfway. The two were pushing the wrong way. The door stuck, locking them inside.

By now, everyone believed the fools had actually been trying to rob the bank. The police were called. Everyone had one more good laugh as they were finally hauled away.

# Grand Theft

One evening in Los Angeles, Mrs. H. Sharpe was taking her dog, Jonathan, for a walk. Mrs. Sharpe, as always, had brought along a pooper-scooper and a plastic bag to clean up after her dog.

The two had a long and pleasant walk. Jonathan had finished his business and Mrs. Sharpe had finished her cleanup. It was getting dark, and the two headed for home. Suddenly, Mrs. Sharpe heard a rustling noise behind her. Frightened, she hurried her pace. But in the next instant a shadowy figure rushed up from behind, snatched Mrs. Sharpe's bag from her hand, and raced off into the darkness.

It wasn't a handbag that the thief got. It was a plastic bag. And you *know* what was in that bag. One can only imagine the look on the thief's face when he looked in the bag to count his loot and discovered what he had stolen.

It would seem that this is one of those rare cases in which the criminal really got what he deserved.

# In the Pen

THE YEAR: 1924. THE PLACE: Pike County, Pennsylvania.

Looking sad-eyed and a bit confused, the prisoner was led into the courtroom. Character witnesses took the stand and testified that the accused was usually well-mannered, fun-loving, and friendly.

But the evidence was clear. The prisoner had committed murder. More witnesses were called. They described the killing in detail. It was an open-and-shut case.

"Guilty!" thundered the judge.

The prisoner hung his head but said nothing. Then he was led away. He was loaded into a paddy wagon and taken to the state penitentiary. The sentence: life in prison.

In 1930, the prisoner died behind bars in the arms of a fellow inmate. Others looked on and wept as he passed away.

On the surface, this would seem to be an ordinary story, an ordinary case. It's not. In fact, it is one of the strangest criminal cases on record. Why? For one reason—the prisoner was a dog!

Pep was a black Labrador retriever. And Pep's crime: he

had killed the cat of the governor of Pennsylvania. The governor loved his cat as though it were a person, and he wanted its killer treated as though human.

The governor was also a judge. He demanded not only that Pep be tried for murder, but that he be tried in his own courtroom. As to a jury, there would be none. The judge would render the verdict. Pep didn't have a chance. The judge had already made up his mind what to do with the dog; and off to prison he went.

Fortunately, our story can end on a happy note. Pep was allowed to wander at will through the prison. When the other prisoners went out on work details, he trotted out with them and kept them company. Everybody liked him, and he liked everybody. He brought joy to his fellow inmates, and he was lavished with love until the day he died.

# Icy Standoff

December 2, 1975, was a freezing cold day in Carson City, Nevada. Harold Hess, a local businessman, had just finished an errand. Making his way back to his car, he was annoyed to find a policeman writing him a parking ticket.

Hess went to the policeman. He explained that he didn't deserve a ticket. He had tried to put money in the parking meter, but it was frozen. Taking out a dime, he showed the policeman that the meter wouldn't work.

The policeman just shrugged. "That's not my problem," he said, handing Mr. Hess the ticket.

Though angry, Mr. Hess decided to pay the fine.

The following day he walked into the courthouse. After waiting his turn, he walked up to a justice of the peace. He smiled and presented the man with a large block of ice. In the center of the frozen block were the ticket and the money to pay the fine.

"Hey, how am I supposed to get that out of there?" demanded the justice of the peace.

Mr. Hess just shrugged. "That's not my problem," he said, and walked out of the room.

# The Cop Who Became His Own Prisoner

---

The rookie police officer was nervous. It was his first day on the job. He had been assigned to traffic patrol.

Only a few minutes had passed before he spotted his first lawbreaker. A man driving a pickup truck breezed through a stop sign. After a brief chase, the officer gained the driver's attention and waved him to the side of the road.

The officer stepped from his car and locked the door. He had not taken two steps before he realized he had left his citation book in the car. Turning back, he discovered something far worse. He had locked his keys in the ignition!

The rookie gave the man in the pickup truck a warning and sent him on his way. He then walked back to the patrol car, climbed into the backseat, and tried to reach through the wire grill to unlock a front door. Just then a car whizzed by, and he slammed the back door to keep it from being hit—locking himself in the prisoner section! He used a portable walkie-talkie to call the chief of police to come and set him free.

# A Lesson in Geography

It happened a few years ago in the town of Santa Fe, Argentina. A man boarded a local bus. He waited for everyone to take their seats. Then, gun in hand, he sneaked up behind the driver. "This is a hijacking!" said the man. "Take me to Cuba!"

"Didn't you ever go to school?" asked the driver.

"Huh?" said the hijacker.

"Well," said the driver, "I can't take you to Cuba."

"And why not?"

"Because Cuba is across the ocean. And this bus doesn't drive on water."

"Oh," said the man. "Guess you better let me off, then."

"No problem," said the driver as he opened the bus door.

The would-be hijacker, gun still in hand, got off the bus. Spotted by police, he was quickly arrested.

# Killer Sues Prison

In 1979, Wally Weed murdered a young minister. He was convicted and sent to Utah State Prison for life.

On a summer day in 1984, Weed and two other men escaped from the prison. All three were captured a few days later.

When Weed was returned to prison, he filed a $2 million lawsuit. He sued the prison *for putting him in danger by letting him escape*!

"I was real afraid the whole time," he complained in the suit. "Mean cops with shotguns were after me. I had to swim through big streams. I got all scratched and bruised. I hurt real bad, and I was all hot and sweaty. Mosquitoes and other bugs bit me all over. It's only fair that they have to pay for what I went through. It's their fault I escaped."

Weed had another demand. He wanted the warden and all the prison guards fired. "They should be punished," he said, "for not doing their jobs very good."

To date, none of Weed's demands regarding the firing of prison personnel have been met. He's still waiting for the outcome of his lawsuit.

In the meantime, he has filed another one. In this suit he complains that he has been put in a cell by himself with a round-the-clock guard. This is unfair, he believes, regardless of the fact that he is in there to make sure he doesn't escape again.

# Accidents and Disasters

# Frozen Alive

It was an icy December morning in 1987. Nine-year-old Justin Bunker climbed from bed and glanced out at the snow-blanketed Connecticut countryside. He dressed, ate a quick breakfast, then made his way across the snow to a friend's house.

The two boys borrowed a sled from a neighbor. Then they headed to the playground of a nearby school. It had a great hill for sledding.

There was a shortcut into the playground. The chain link fence around an outdoor swimming pool had an opening in it. The boys climbed through. They were making their way around the iced-over pool, but it was just too tempting. Justin and his friend skated out onto the thick ice in their boots. The two began horsing around. That's when it happened.

Without warning, the ice gave way under Justin's feet. He let out a yell as he shot down into the freezing cold water. His friend watched helplessly. He stared down into the dark hole through which Justin had fallen. Justin appeared to be on the bottom, face-up and not moving.

In a state of panic, the boy raced to Justin's mother, who called the fire department. Within six minutes, firemen and paramedics arrived at the scene. Two of them immediately jumped into the frozen pool. Their heavy clothing and the darkness of the icy water made it hard to move rapidly. Several minutes passed before they reached the apparently lifeless body.

Finally, Justin was dragged from the pool. But there was no hope. He had been completely underwater for over twenty minutes. His eyes were frozen shut. His lungs and stomach were partly filled with ice-cold water. His body was stiff.

Justin was dead—almost.

Paramedics worked on him as they rushed him off in an ambulance. When he reached the hospital, he was unconscious and unable to breathe on his own. But he did have a faint pulse.

Doctors wrapped him in an electric heating pad. An oxygen mask was strapped over his face. For eight hours he lay in a hospital bed, unmoving, seemingly lifeless.

Suddenly he sat up in bed! Two nurses rushed to him. He pulled off the oxygen mask and tried to struggle free of the electric blanket. The nurses held his arms and tried to calm him. "Let go of me," he demanded. "What's going on? What happened?"

A few weeks later, Justin went home. He was healthy and normal in every way.

The obvious question is, how could someone be completely underwater for more than twenty minutes and still live? It seems impossible, but the same thing has happened to quite a few people. Justin's case is simply one of the most dramatic ones.

When someone plunges into freezing water, he or she may be "quick-frozen." Blood vessels near the skin shut down. The brain and other organs cool rapidly and need very little oxygen. The heart beats very slowly, and may even stop. Basically, the person is in a state of suspended animation.

That is what happened to Justin Bunker. And that is why he is alive and well today.

# Fall Out, Fall In

On a September day in 1918, two Canadian airmen were on a training mission. At the controls of the open-cockpit biplane was George Makepiece. His passenger was Captain J. H. Sedley. Neither man wore a parachute or seat belt.

Pilot Makepiece cruised at a high altitude for a time. Suddenly he went into a steep dive. In the process, Sedley fell out of the plane.

Makepiece brought the plane out of its dive and leveled off several hundred feet below. High above, he could see Sedley free-falling. There was nothing the pilot could do. Sedley was falling to his death.

Makepiece lost sight of the man. Suddenly he was startled by a loud thump near the tail of the plane. He looked back and was shocked to see Sedley! Somehow the falling man had landed back on the plane!

For several minutes Sedley held on for dear life. Then slowly he climbed back into his seat.

A short time later the plane landed safely. Both men were speechless but unhurt.

# A Favor Returned

It was a summer day in 1965. Four-year-old Roger Lausier was having a grand time. His parents had taken him to a beach near Salem, Massachusetts. He made sand castles. Then he waded out into the water. There was a sudden drop-off in the footing below, and little Roger was suddenly over his head. He didn't know how to swim. He tried to cry out, and sucked water into his lungs.

The little boy knew he was drowning. But a moment later, strong arms were around him. Then a woman was carrying him to shore.

Roger's mother was crying. Both she and her husband blamed themselves for taking their eyes off their son—if only for an instant. They thanked the woman again and again.

Her name was Alice Blaise.

Nine years later Roger returned to the same beach. He was now thirteen. He was big and strong for his age, and a good swimmer.

Spreading his towel on the sand, he suddenly heard a

shout. It was a cry for help. Beyond the breakers he could see a man fighting for his life.

Roger grabbed an air raft and quickly paddled out to the man. He reached him not a moment too soon. Roger helped the man onto the raft. Then, sliding into the water, he towed him to shore.

Later, Roger learned something very interesting about the man. His last name was Blaise. His wife was Alice—Alice Blaise, the woman who had saved Roger from drowning nine years before on the exact same beach.

# Tidal Wave!

It happened in north Boston, on January 15, 1919. It was a few minutes after noon. No one had any idea of what was coming their way.

Workers were busy down by the docks and in warehouses. Horse-drawn carts clattered through the streets. Model T Fords chugged along, hooted horns. People strolled.

It hit suddenly, with almost no warning. There was a deep rumbling noise. Then a tidal wave two stories high slammed into the city.

Houses and buildings shattered. The Boston Fire Station was lifted from its foundation. Firemen were crushed and drowned as the station crashed into the harbor.

At a park, many workers had just settled down to eat lunch. Some never even saw the wave coming. They drowned where they sat.

An elevated train track collapsed. Train cars were picked up and thrown about like toys.

Neither horses, cars, nor people on foot could outrun the monster wave. It caught up to them, swallowed them up, carried them away.

In all, 21 persons died and more than 150 were injured—by the strangest tidal wave in history.

It was not a wave of water.

At the Purity Distilling Company a huge cast-iron tank had rumbled its low warning. Then it had burst open, releasing a great wave of raw black *molasses*!

Two million gallons of the sweet, sticky syrup had swept through north Boston. Sightseers who came later couldn't help but walk in the stuff. On their way home they tracked the goo throughout the city. Boston smelled of molasses for weeks. The harbor ran brown until summer.

# A Miracle

It was the night of July 25, 1956. Slender, brown-haired, 14-year-old Linda Morgan was on board the passenger liner *Andrea Doria*, which was headed from Italy to New York. After dinner and a walk with her mother, Linda decided to turn in early. She made her way to her cabin, changed into her nightgown, and was soon fast asleep in her bunk.

Linda could not have known it, but bearing down on the *Andrea Doria* in the fog was the Swedish liner *Stockholm*. At the last moment, the captains of the ships tried to steer away from each other. It was too late. The *Stockholm* rammed into the *Andrea Doria*, tearing a 40-foot gash in its side.

The bow of the *Stockholm* sliced right through Linda Morgan's cabin. Nothing was left of it. The ship stopped. Then it went into reverse, pulling its bow out of the side of the *Andrea Doria*.

Hours passed.

The *Andrea Doria* was sinking. Its passengers were being rescued. The bow of the *Stockholm* was crushed, but the ship was still seaworthy.

Bernabé Garcia, a sailor aboard the *Stockholm*, was checking the damage to the bow. Suddenly he heard a cry for help. He made his way through the wreckage. He found a teenage girl. She was in a smashed bed on a mattress.

"What is your name?" asked Garcia.

"Linda Morgan," was the reply. "Where am I? What ship is this? What's going on?"

It was a while before anyone was able to figure out what had happened. The bow of the *Stockholm* had ripped into Linda's cabin, directly under her bunk. She was knocked out by a blow to the head. Then the ship had pulled back. As it did, it carried Linda, still in her bed, back out with it. Hours later she awoke on the bow of the *Stockholm*, miles away from the sinking *Andrea Doria*.

Linda was later taken to a hospital. She had three broken bones and other injuries, but she was going to be okay. Bernabé Garcia, who had first found her, came to visit. He smiled and touched her on the cheek. "It is a miracle," he whispered. "A miracle."

# Art and Literature

# Baseball Wasn't His Thing

"Take me out to the ball game,
Take me out with the crowd,
Buy me some peanuts and Cracker Jacks,
I don't care if I never get back."

Songwriter Jack Norworth wrote the greatly popular "Take Me Out to the Ball Game" in 1908. Incredibly, he didn't see his first baseball game till thirty-four years later, in 1942!

Norworth was on a New York City subway train when he spotted an ad for the old New York Giants baseball team. He found a pencil and a scrap of paper in his pocket and started scribbling. Thirty minutes later he'd finished the song.

In later years, Norworth joked that he had written "more than 3,000 songs, seven of them good." His big hits included not only "Take Me Out to the Ball Game," but also "Shine on Harvest Moon" and "Meet Me in Apple Blossom Time."

But how come Norworth had written such a famous song

about "America's favorite pastime" but had taken so long to be taken out to a ball game? When asked the question, he said, "So what? I'm a songwriter. That's what I like to do. Going to baseball games doesn't interest me a bit."

# The E-less Novel

*E* is the most often used letter in the English language. In fact, *E* appears in so many words that it is difficult to write even one sentence without using one.

In Britain in 1939 author Ernest Vincent Wright published a novel entitled *Gadsby*. The strange thing about the book is that it is *E*-less. It has more than 50,000 words, none of which contains an *E*.

Surprisingly, *Gadsby* reads smoothly and well. The *E*s are hardly missed. Here is a sample passage from the work:

> Gadsby was walking back from a visit down in Branton on a Saturday night. Coming to Broadway, a booming bass drum and sounds of singing told of a small Salvation Army unit carrying on amidst Broadway's night shopping crowds.

Writing an E-less book must have been very hard. And the author did a good job. The only question is, why did he do it? What made him want to do something so odd? Perhaps the answer is simple. Maybe he just wanted to find out for himself if it could be done.

# The Longest Painting

In the nineteenth century, artist John Banvard decided to do a painting of the Mississippi River. The result was not something you could hang on your wall. It was three miles long!

Banvard worked for years on the painting. In 1845, it was finally finished and put on display in Louisville, Kentucky. It was exhibited like a giant scroll. Showing scenes from along the Mississippi, it was unrolled from one huge spindle to another.

Banvard took his painting on tour throughout the United States and England. It is said that it was not an especially good painting, but people enjoyed it. The tours made Banvard a small fortune.

When the artist died, the painting was cut into sections. For many years, parts of it were used as backdrops in theaters.

# Portrait of Death

Andre Marcellin was a painter who began work in 1907 in Paris. He did beautiful landscapes. People would often ask him to do portraits. Always, he would refuse. "I do not know why," he would say, "but for some reason I am afraid to do them."

A Paris banker kept after Marcellin. Finally, he got the artist to agree to do his portrait. Proudly, the banker sat as Marcellin worked.

Two days after the portrait was finished, the banker died.

Marcellin did not paint another portrait for six months. Then he felt the need to do another. A woman came to him and asked to have her picture done.

Again, two days later, the woman was dead.

It must be coincidence, Marcellin told himself. Wanting to prove this, he painted the likeness of another client. The man was a close friend.

The portrait was finished and paid for. The friend took it home.

Two days passed. Nothing happened. Marcellin breathed a sigh of relief. On the third day came the news. Marcellin's

friend had died that morning, suddenly and unexpectedly.

Marcellin was sure now that his paintings were cursed. He vowed never to paint another portrait.

For five years he kept good his vow.

In 1913, he met a lovely woman, Francois Noel. The two became engaged. Francois begged him to do her portrait. Marcellin refused. He told her of the curse. She laughed and said it was nothing but foolishness. Still, he refused.

As the months passed, Francois kept pestering him to do a painting of her. Everyday she became more and more angry. Finally, she told him he had to do her portrait. If he did not, then she would not marry him.

Marcellin gave in. He did the portrait. A week later, Francois died.

Marcellin was filled with sadness and guilt. For weeks he sat alone in his studio, doing nothing. Finally, he made a decision. He started work on another picture.

This one was of himself.

A few days after it was finished, Andre Marcellin was dead.

# The $5,216 Fine for an Overdue Book

It was a spring day in the year 1984. Sixty-five-year-old Chet Hanchett quietly entered the Modesto High School library. Sheepishly, he made his way to the librarian's desk.

"I have a book to return," he said. "I'm afraid it's a bit overdue."

"How many days?" asked the woman.

"Not days—*years*," said Mr. Hanchett, placing a copy of Robert Louis Stevenson's *Kidnapped* on the desk.

The librarian opened the book. "Good heavens!" she said. "This book was checked out in 1934! It's fifty years overdue!"

Mr. Hanchett nodded.

The librarian went to work with a pocket calculator. When all was added up, the overdue fine came to $5,216.

Mr. Hanchett then said he found the book high up on a shelf. He had no idea as to how it came to be there. The last person listed as having checked it out was a high school friend.

The librarian smiled. She told Mr. Hanchett to forget the fine, and thanked him for returning the book.

# A Book That Foretold the Future

In 1898, an English author named Morgan Robertson published a novel about a huge new ocean liner. The ship was far larger than any that had ever been built. The fictional characters on board were mostly the rich and famous. The ship set off on its first voyage. Halfway across the Atlantic, on a cold night in April, the make-believe ship hit an iceberg and sank. There was great loss of life.

Robertson's book, entitled *Futility*, did not do well. Few people read it. Few people even knew about it.

Certainly not the owners of the White Star Shipping Line.

Fourteen years after the publication of the book, White Star built what was then the largest ocean liner in the world. In nearly every way, it was almost exactly like the one in Robertson's novel. Both were around 800 feet long and weighed between 60 and 70 thousand tons. Both vessels had triple propellers and could make 24 to 25 knots. Both could carry about 3,000 people, and both had enough lifeboats for only a fraction of this number. But, then, this wasn't supposed to matter; both ships were said to be "unsinkable."

On April 10, 1912, the real ship left England on her first voyage. On board were some of the richest and most famous people in the world. On a cold April night, about halfway across the Atlantic, the ship struck an iceberg. With great loss of life, she sank.

The real ship, of course, was the *Titanic*. As for the name of the imaginary ship, the author called it the *Titan*.

# Science

# How Many Hours in a Day?

Everyone knows there are 24 hours in a day. But scientists say that days will be much longer in the future.

Ten billion years from now the length of a day on earth will increase from 24 hours to 564 hours! And 20 billion years from now a day will be at least 1,128 hours long.

Scientists say it is the force of the ocean tides that will make the days longer. Tides are gradually slowing the rotation of the earth. The more slowly the earth turns, the longer the days become.

Scientists also say that one of our days at present is six times longer than a day was when the earth was first formed. Though it may be hard to believe, a day on earth was originally only four hours long!

# Frog in a Rock

On February 2, 1958, four men were at work in a mine in Utah. They hacked their way through eight feet of sandstone, then they came up against a fossilized tree trunk. The only way they could break it up and get it out of the way was by blasting.

The explosion cracked open the rock-hard trunk. The men went to carry away the broken slabs and pieces—and got the biggest surprise of their lives. In the center of the fossilized wood was a smoothly rounded hole about the size of an egg. And inside the hole was a tiny frog. It was shriveled and grayish-brown. Its toes were long but not webbed, and there were tiny suction cups on the ends of its fingers.

The creature lived for 28 hours after being released from the stony prison that had held it for ages.

Scientists studied the frog. No other like it was on earth. However, it was quite possible, they said, that such a frog had existed in prehistoric times.

But how did the frog come to be inside the rounded hole? It could not have crawled in through fossilized wood.

There were no gaps of any kind leading into the hole. It was a tightly sealed compartment.

To the scientists, the frog seemed to be a prehistoric creature. And it looked as old and dried up as the tree in which it was found, as though it had been trapped in there for centuries. But if so, then how could it still be alive?

It is one of the strangest cases in the history of science. So far, no one has been able to explain it.

# The Human Radio

He thought he was going crazy.

Not long ago in Bridgeport, Connecticut, a factory worker was sure he was losing his mind. Everyday for weeks, he kept hearing music and little voices in his head. No matter where he went, the voices and music would follow him. He would even hear them in his sleep.

The man went to a doctor. It took a while, but the doctor found the problem.

A few weeks before, the man had had some dental work done. Accidentally, several little chunks of silver had gotten stuck between his teeth. The silver particles were picking up radio signals. The signals were then sent through the bones of his face to his brain. In effect, the man had been turned into a human radio receiver.

The doctor removed the bits of silver, and the man was cured.

# A Comical Idea

One day in 1964, a freighter was entering the harbor of Kuwait. On board were 6,000 sheep. The ship was having problems. It was taking on water. Suddenly, it flipped over and sank.

Most of the crew escaped. All of the sheep went down with the ship.

The people living near the harbor were worried. Trapped inside the ship were thousands of sheep. As they rotted, the harbor would become badly polluted. The smell would be terrible.

A Danish man by the name of Karl Kroyer happened to be in town. Kroyer was not an engineer. But he did have an idea as to how to raise the ship.

At first, everybody thought his idea was silly. Kroyer suggested filling the inside of the ship with Ping-Pong balls. The air in them, he believed, would bring up the sunken freighter.

No one had a better idea.

A ship was sent to Kuwait Harbor. It carried 30 *billion* specially made plastic balls. They were like Ping-Pong balls, only much smaller, about the size of large pearls. The ship was also armed with a long injector hose. Divers took the hose down to the sunken freighter and injected the balls into the hull. At first, nothing happened. Then slowly but surely, the freighter rose to the surface.

Everyone thought Kroyer was a genius. It was such a great idea! How had he thought of it?

Kroyer laughed. Then he explained where the idea had come from. As a boy, he had loved comic books. One of those he had never forgotten was a Donald Duck story. In the story, Donald is on a boat with his nephews Huey, Dewey, and Louie. When the boat sinks, Donald and his nephews raise it, using Ping-Pong balls.

It had only been a silly, funny idea in a comic book. Funnily enough, the idea worked in real life—just as it had on paper for a bunch of make-believe ducks.

# The Woman Who Couldn't Sleep

Like most people, you sleep about eight hours a day. In a year, then, you sleep 2,920 hours, and in thirty years, this comes to a staggering 87,600 hours!

For Mrs. Ines Fernandez of Seville, Spain, things were different. For the last thirty years or more of her life, she *never* slept—not for even an hour!

It all started on a warm summer afternoon long ago.

Mrs. Fernandez and her two children were standing in the open doorway of their house. A parade was going by. The children were jumping up and down with excitement. Mrs. Fernandez was a bit tired and bored.

"I yawned," said the woman. "And suddenly a horrible pain went through my head. Within a few hours the pain was gone. That night I went to bed, but I couldn't sleep. The next night the same thing happened. And the next, and the next, and the next. I've been that way ever since. I can rest, but I can never fall asleep. For over thirty years this has gone on."

Mrs. Fernandez went to many doctors. She took, she said, "thousands of pills." But neither the doctors nor the pills were of any help. Nothing could put her to sleep.

All in all, for the last thirty years or so of her life, Mrs. Fernandez was in good health. But she was always tired. "I am so tired," she would complain. "So very, very tired."

Each night, Ines Fernandez would put on a nightgown. But she had long ago given up on going to bed. Instead, she would sit down in a chair. And there she would wait—not for sleep, but for morning to come.

After more than thirty years of this strange torture, Mrs. Fernandez passed away. At long last, the sleepless woman was laid to rest.

# Politics and Government

# The Foot Powder Mayor

The year was 1969. The town of Picoaza, Ecuador, had a rather unusual problem. The town council was embarrassed. They didn't know what to do. The people had just elected a new mayor—one that came in a can.

The new mayor of Picoaza was a brand of foot powder!

This is how it happened.

The Pulvapies foot powder company decided to make the most of an upcoming election. It ran ads that sounded like their product was a person running for office. The ads were the same size, shape, and color of real ballots. Across the top were the words, VOTE FOR PULVAPIES.

The votes were counted. To everyone's surprise, Pulvapies had won by a landslide! A foot powder was the new mayor!

Red-faced election officials explained to the people what had happened. Then they got a court order to keep the foot powder mayor from being installed in office. Finally, new elections were held.

A man won.

He wasn't very popular. In fact, he wasn't liked at all. Signs began appearing. BRING BACK PULVAPIES! they read. PULVAPIES, THE BEST MAYOR WE EVER HAD!

# Law Going Nowhere

In 1971, the town leaders of Harbor Springs, Michigan, voted to lower the age for cab drivers. The age requirement was dropped from 21 to 18.

Many people were upset about the law, but not because younger people would be able to drive taxicabs.

"It's the silliest thing I've ever heard of," said one man. "The law just doesn't make any sense."

He was right. Lowering the age for taxi drivers made no sense at all. Why? For the simple reason that Harbor Springs lacked something. It didn't have any taxis. Not one.

# The Do-nothing Congressman

The year was 1868. Thaddeus Stevens from Pennsylvania had been nominated by the Republican Party to run for office.

Republicans, of course, hoped Stevens would win.

The Democrats, naturally, wanted him to lose. In fact, they were especially nasty about Stevens' nomination. They said nominating him was stupid. He was a joke. He couldn't possibly do the job.

In November, the election was held. Stevens won by a landslide.

As it turned out, the Democrats were right about Stevens. He wasn't much of a Congressman. He never made any speeches. He wasn't on any committees. In fact, not once did he even show up for a congressional session!

Of course, no one expected him to. Not even the Republicans were surprised at Stevens' conduct. After all, they had only nominated him because they liked him, not because they thought he would do a good job. And how could he?

He was dead!

Thaddeus Stevens had long been a respected politician. In August, 1868, he died. Soon after his burial, he was nominated by his party as a "fitting tribute" to his memory. Three months later he was elected.

And for the next two years the United States had a dead Congressman.

# Señor Banana

In 1974, Señor José Ramon del Cuet threw in the towel as mayor of the little town of Coacaloco, Mexico. Señor Cuet had a little help in making his decision. Four thousand citizens made it very clear they wanted him to go.

The people of Coacaloco made their living raising bananas. For years, the mayor had been lining his pockets. Large sums of money coming in from banana sales kept disappearing. The people got poorer and poorer. Señor Cuet got richer and richer.

Finally, the people were fed up. Four thousand strong, they stormed the town hall. Running from room to room, they finally found the mayor. He was hiding under a desk.

They pulled him out and sat him down. They demanded that he resign.

He refused. He said he was a good man, an innocent man. "Please, my friends, believe me."

A box of bananas was brought in. Then, one after the other, Mayor Cuet was forced to eat them.

Even a man who loves bananas has his limit. Finally, Cuet reached his. After all, twelve pounds of bananas *is* a lot to swallow.

Not feeling his best, Mayor Cuet took pen in hand and signed his resignation. Then he staggered away, out of the banana business forever.

# King Henry I of America

Imagine opening a U.S. history book, and our first president isn't mentioned. But there *is* a lot about our *first king*—King Henry I of America!

The United States, of course, has never had a king. But we almost did.

It happened like this.

In 1783, the Revolutionary War came to an end. The colonies had finally won their freedom from British rule. What the new nation needed was a leader. But who should this person be? No one was sure. Debate on the question went on and on.

Three years passed. Still, no decision had been made.

Finally, a group of American statesmen got together. In the group were Alexander Hamilton, James Monroe, and Nathaniel Gorham. After many days of discussion, it was decided that what the United States needed was a king. And this man, they agreed, should come from one of the royal families of Europe.

Several names were brought up. After all had been discussed, it was decided that 50-year-old Prince Henry of

KING OF
THE UNITED STATES OF AMERICA

Prussia was the best man for the job. A few days later they sent him a long letter. It asked that he become "King of the American Colonies."

At first, Henry was excited about the idea. Then he had second thoughts. He wasn't sure he wanted to leave Europe or take a chance on being the ruler of such a wild and unsettled land. Then he changed his mind again. He sat down to write a letter accepting the offer.

He tore up the letter. He wanted more time to think.

Months passed. Finally, Henry did send off a letter. But all it said was that he wasn't quite sure what he wanted to do.

The letter not only annoyed the Americans, it also caused *them* to have second thoughts. What kind of a leader would Henry make? Did they really want a king who couldn't even decide whether or not he wanted to be king?

After more thinking and talking, everyone agreed to forget not only about Henry but also about having a king. Instead, there would be an elected president.

The rest is history.

But what if Prince Henry had said yes to the offer? If he had, all of U.S. history would be changed. Today, instead of an elected president, the country would be ruled by a king or queen, the descendant of a now-forgotten prince who had trouble making up his mind.

# The Unknown and Mysterious

# Into Thin Air

It was the morning of September 23, 1880. On a small farm in Tennessee, David Lang and his wife were sitting on their porch. Their two children, George, 8, and Sarah, 11, were playing in the yard.

David Lang spotted two friends driving toward the farm in a buggy. He waved and headed across an open field to greet them. Suddenly he looked back at his family. Something was wrong. He seemed confused and in pain.

That's when it happened.

Standing in the middle of an open field, David Lang vanished into thin air!

His family and two friends rushed to the spot. They thought perhaps he had fallen into a hole or a crack in the ground. But there were none. The spot was nothing but flat, solid land. Sobbing and screaming, Mrs. Lang was led back to the house.

The sheriff came. Neighbors came. Dozens of people searched the field and nearby land. Even scientists were called in. They studied the area but could find nothing to explain what had happened. David Lang was simply gone.

For months the search went on. Curiosity seekers came to gawk. All the Lang servants and farmhands quit in fear.

When spring came, another strange thing happened. The grass in the spot where Lang had disappeared grew in a tall circle of green. The farm animals were afraid of the place. Not one of them would enter the circle.

One day in August, 1881, Lang's two children approached the circle of high grass. Sarah called out, "Father, where are you?" There was no answer. She repeated the question several more times. They were about to walk away. Suddenly they heard a faint cry. It was a cry for help that came from nowhere.

Quickly the children ran and got their mother. She returned with them to the spot. Mrs. Lang called out as the children had done. *Her husband answered!* For several days the family returned. Each day when they called, the answering voice became weaker. Finally, there was no answer at all.

More than a hundred years have passed. Still, the mystery goes on. What happened to David Lang? People have come up with many ideas. Some believe he went into another dimension. Others think he was picked up by a UFO invisible to the human eye. But no one knows. No one really knows how or why David Lang walked into a field one day—and disappeared forever off the face of the earth.

# Water from Nowhere

In 1972, nine-year-old Eugenio Rossi was taken to a hospital on the island of Sardinia. Doctors who examined the sick boy found that he had a problem with his liver.

Eugenio was taken to a ward, a hospital room containing many patients. Nurses put the boy to bed to await treatment. But shortly after he got into bed, an odd thing began to happen. Water started to flow up through the floor in the room.

"It was coming up everywhere," said a nurse. "It wasn't like some sort of ordinary leak. It was as though water was being squeezed out of all the floorboards."

Plumbers were called. They searched carefully, but there was nothing wrong with any of the pipes.

Meanwhile, one by one, the patients were taken out of the ward. Finally, Eugenio's turn came. As he was wheeled out of the room, the flooding stopped!

He was put into another ward. And almost as soon as he entered the new room, water began to seep up through the floor there, too!

The nurses quickly took him out. This time he was put

in a room by himself. The same thing began to happen. But at least now the flooding wasn't bothering other patients.

Doctors began treating the boy. A clean-up crew had to work around the clock. As the doctors took care of Eugenio, the workers endlessly mopped up the floor.

As the days passed, Eugenio started getting better. As he did, the flow of water slowed down. Finally, his liver problem was cured. The flooding stopped completely.

It seems there was a connection between the boy's illness and the water that came up from nowhere. But what that connection might have been is anybody's guess.

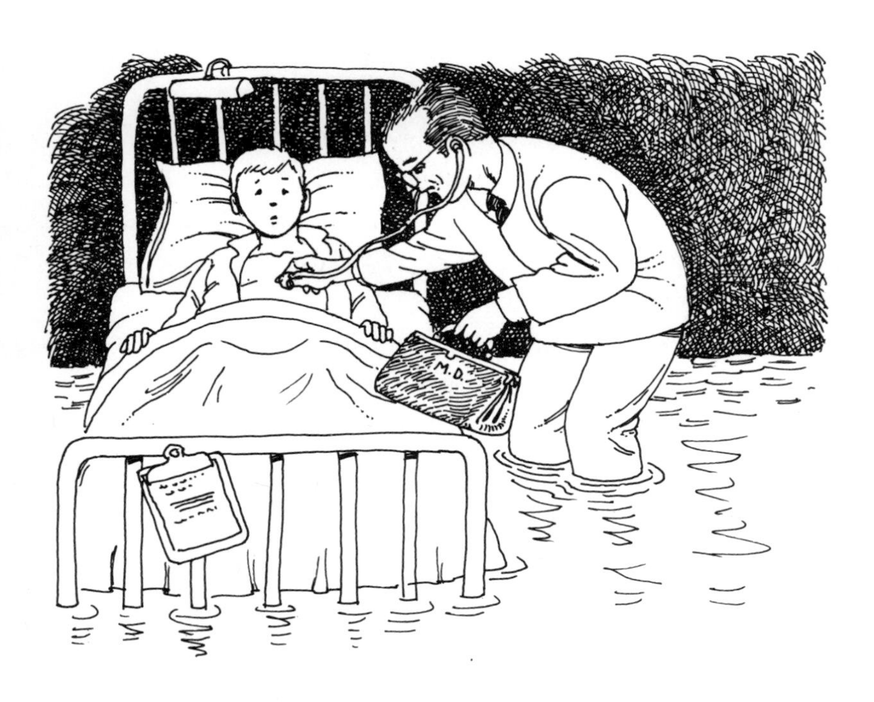

# Message from the Grave?

Several years ago a North Carolina man, David Holt, passed away. His death was sudden and unexpected. His wife was left with almost no money and a four-year-old son to support.

Two weeks after the funeral, little Bobby Holt was sitting at the kitchen table. He was drawing pictures. Suddenly he pushed his drawings away. He took several sheets of clean paper and began to write. After filling three pages, he gave the message to his mother.

Mrs. Holt couldn't believe what she saw. The message was in shorthand. Young Bobby couldn't read or write, let alone use shorthand!

Not knowing shorthand herself, Mrs. Holt took the sheets to an expert. When the message was read, Mrs. Holt almost fainted.

It was from her husband! It told how much he loved his wife and son and how much he *missed* them. It also said they should go to a bank in New York.

Mrs. Holt was upset by the message. And the part about the bank puzzled her completely. She had never heard of the bank. She could think of no reason why she should go there.

Still, she did what the message had told her to do. She and Bobby packed their things and took the train to New York.

At the bank, Mrs. Holt talked to the manager. He told her that her husband had rented a safety deposit box long ago.

The box was opened. In it was a little cash. More important, there was a life insurance policy worth thousands of dollars. Never again would the young widow have to worry about money!

A story such as this is hard to explain. Did young Bobby somehow receive a message from the grave? If not, then how could he suddenly start writing shorthand? How and why was he able to locate the insurance money—money that only a dead man knew about?

# The Electric Lady

THE DATE: November, 1967. THE PLACE: A lawyer's office in Rosenheim, Germany.

Everyone was going crazy. The world was going crazy. No one in the office could believe what was going on.

It had started on the morning of November 3, a Monday. Suddenly a neon lighting tube fell to the floor and shattered. No one knew why it had come loose. Still, it didn't seem like anything of real importance. The tube was replaced and everyone went back to work.

The next day the same thing happened. Again the tube was replaced. A moment later it began unscrewing itself! And so did all the other neon tubes! The clerks stared in amazement as the tubes went around and around without being touched. Then they took cover as the tubes came crashing down.

An electrician was called. He decided something must be wrong with the neon lighting system. He took it out and replaced it with one that used ordinary bulbs. When he was done, he turned on the lights. The new system seemed to work fine. The electrician left. Again, everyone settled down to work.

An hour passed. Suddenly, one of the light bulbs burst with a loud pop. Then, one after the other, all the bulbs exploded!

Again, the electrician was called. He had no idea of what was wrong. He turned off all the light switches. He left, promising to come back in the morning.

No sooner was he out the door than all the switches started going wild. Over and over, they flipped on and off. And no one was touching them!

But that wasn't the only problem. Already the photocopier was doing all sorts of odd things. Weird noises were coming from inside it. Then, without anyone touching it, it started up on its own. Suddenly, it broke down completely. Photocopy fluid spurted out all over the floor.

The machine was unplugged. The spilled fluid was cleaned up. For a moment, everything seemed to have returned to normal. Even the light switches had stopped acting up.

That's when all the telephones in the office started ringing. Over and over, clerks answered the phones. But there was no one there! As soon as a phone was hung up, it would ring again.

The phones were taken off their hooks. That should have solved the problem. It didn't. The phones started dialing numbers by themselves!

At this point, there was nothing that could be done except close down the office.

The office manager called the power company. They checked every part of the electrical system. Nothing seemed to be wrong with it. There was nothing that could explain all the crazy things that had happened.

The manager also talked to the police. They thought someone was playing some kind of a trick. But how such a trick could be pulled off, they had no idea.

The police questioned all the people who worked at the office. All were very puzzled—and a little frightened—by what had happened.

A 19-year-old clerk named Ann-Marie seemed most frightened of all. She had just started working at the office—on Monday. The job was new to her. She had been

very nervous. Then all the strange things started happening, and she had gotten even more scared. Now, worst of all, she had to talk to the police.

She was very tense as she walked into the room where the policeman waited. He asked his first question. Suddenly, the lights in the room started going off and on! File cabinet drawers opened by themselves! In tears, Ann-Marie ran from the room.

Somehow, it had been this young lady who had been causing all the impossible happenings. No one knew why, and certainly not Ann-Marie.

Doctors examined her. They could find nothing wrong with her, nothing ordinary. But tests showed that her body seemed charged with electricity. The electric charges became very strong when she was nervous.

She was given pills to relax her. Then she was taken to her parents' home to rest. But even there, the same sort of strange things happened.

As the weeks passed, the odd happenings slowly stopped. Ann-Marie got another job. Her first day there, it all started up again. She quit the job a few hours after starting.

Ann-Marie and her parents moved to a new home. It had no electricity. Her life became quiet and peaceful.

There have been a few other people like Ann-Marie. These people also give off an electric charge. But never has the charge been so powerful or caused so many wild things to happen. Her case is the most ususual one on record.

# The Floating Man

He was known as Joseph of Copertino. Joseph was an Italian priest who was later made a saint by the Catholic Church. If what most history books tell us of his life is true, Joseph was one of the strangest men who ever lived.

Let's start at the end, with Joseph's death in 1663. Shortly before he died, it is said, Joseph rose into the air. Then he floated from his bed to a nearby chapel!

That was the last time Joseph flew.

The first was in 1629. Joseph was in church praying. He went into a trance. Suddenly he let out a shriek and rose into the air. As others in the church stared in disbelief, he slowly drifted down the aisle with his hands outstretched. He landed atop the church altar. On his knees and still in a trance, he continued to pray.

In the years that followed, Joseph flew many more times.

Once he visitied Rome to meet the Pope. Seeing the Pope seemed to fill Joseph with joy. He went into a trance and rose into the air. He stood suspended off the floor for several minutes. The Pope and others begged Joseph to come down. After he had, the Pope ordered that a written record be made of the seemingly impossible thing that had just happened.

Another time, Joseph went to the home of a sick man. While the ailing man looked on, Joseph floated around the room and prayed for his recovery.

Joseph was even able to lift others into the air. One time he grabbed a madman by the hair and rose high above the streets of the town with him. Fifteen minutes passed before the two returned to the ground. When they did, the madman was cured. There were dozens of onlookers. Many fainted at the sight of what they had seen.

Naturally, all that you have just read is hard to believe. But hundreds of people between the years 1629 and 1663 claimed they saw him do it. With their own eyes, they saw Joseph of Copertino fly.

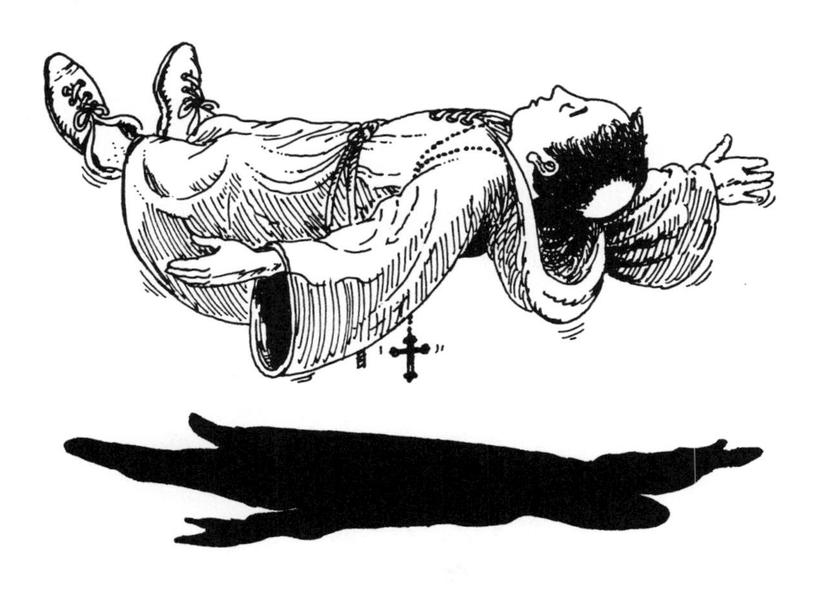

# A Dream Come True

The date was May 7, 1915. Marion Holbourne was sitting in an easy chair in her home in London, England. She dozed off and had a very strange dream.

She dreamed she was on a sinking ship. The vessel was listing badly. Lifeboats were being lowered. Smoke filled the air. Frightened passengers and crewmen rushed about everywhere.

In her dream, Mrs. Holbourne was standing on the upper deck of the ship. She was not worried about her own safety. She was worried about her husband. He was a passenger on the ship, and she couldn't find him.

She spotted an officer, a young man with blond hair and brown eyes. She went up to him and asked about her husband.

The officer in the dream told Mrs. Holbourne that her husband was safe. "He's alive and well," said the officer. "I found him and helped him into a lifeboat."

With that, Mrs. Holbourne suddenly awoke. The dream frightened her terribly, for her husband at the moment actually was traveling at sea. He was on a British passenger liner called the *Lusitania.*

Upset, Mrs. Holbourne told her dream to her family. They laughed it off. "Just a silly nightmare," they told her. "Nothing to worry about."

A few hours later their views quickly changed. News came that the *Lusitania* had been torpedoed by a German submarine. Nearly 1,200 people had perished in the sinking.

But not Mr. Holbourne. One of the lucky survivors, he returned home to his wife and family.

"I owe my life to a young officer," said Mr. Holbourne. "For a while there I was sure I was going to die. The ship was sinking fast. There was smoke everywhere. But then this officer came to my rescue. He got me to a lifeboat just before the ship went down."

Mrs. Holbourne went pale as a ghost. "What did he look like?" she asked. "Do you remember?"

"Never forget him. A nice young bloke. Had blond hair and brown eyes."

Mrs. Holbourne was speechless. Her dream, down to the last detail, had come true.

# Coming Home

This is one of the strangest stories you will ever read. It is the story of the life and death of Charles Coghlan.

Charles Coghlan was born in 1841 on Prince Edward Island. The island is off the coast of Canada. Charles came from a poor family. They did not have enough money to send him to college. But Charles was very bright and well-liked. Neighbors of the Coghlans took up a collection. With the money, Charles was sent to a college in England. He graduated with honors.

Charles returned home. He told his family he wanted to become an actor. His parents were very much against the idea. They said he was not cut out to be an actor. They told him to put such a foolish idea out of his head. And if he did not, they would have nothing to do with him. He would no longer be part of the family.

Charles and his parents argued. Neither side would budge. Finally, Charles decided to leave home. He told his parents they were terribly unfair. He told them that someday he would return to Prince Edward Island. And when he did he would be a famous actor.

At first, it seemed to Charles that maybe his parents had been right. He traveled from town to town in Canada. He did get a few jobs acting in plays, but they were always very small parts.

After several years, he headed south, to the United States. There, his career began to take off. He started getting bigger and better parts. Eventually he was playing the leading role in important plays in cities all across the country. Charles' dream was coming true. Through hard work, he was becoming a rich and famous actor.

One day Charles visited a gypsy fortune-teller. She told him that he would die at the height of his fame. His death would be swift. Also, she said, it would happen in an American southern city. He would be buried there. Still, he would have no rest until he returned to the place of his birth, Prince Edward Island.

The fortune-teller's words bothered Charles. He often told his friends what she had said.

The years passed. Charles Coghlan's fame grew. People came from all over to see him perform. He was thought of as one of the most brilliant actors of his time.

In 1898, he was playing Hamlet in a southern city, Galveston, Texas. One night he suddenly grabbed at his chest. He took a few steps. Then he collapsed on stage. Other actors and people from the audience rushed to help him. But there was nothing they could do. Charles Coghlan, age 57, was dead of a heart attack.

He was buried in the Galveston cemetery.

Two years later a great hurricane roared through the

South. Galveston was especially hard-hit. Buildings were torn to pieces. Ships and boats were sunk. Much of the city was flooded.

Even the Galveston cemetery was not spared. Great waves pounded it. Bodies and coffins by the hundreds were swept away.

The storm finally passed. Friends of Charles Coghlan searched the ruined cemetery. His grave had been washed away. Not a trace of it or his coffin could be found.

In October, 1908, eight years after the hurricane, some fishermen on Prince Edward Island spotted a large box. It was floating in shallow water. The box was old and covered with moss and barnacles. The fishermen waded out to the box. They dragged it ashore and pried it open. In the box was a coffin, and in the coffin was the body of Charles Coghlan!

Somehow, it had all happened. Charles Coghlan had become a famous actor. Later, as the fortune-teller had said he would, he had died at the height of his fame in a southern city. Then he had returned home. In his coffin, he had traveled three thousand miles from the place he had been buried.

Charles Coghlan—brought home by the sea—was finally laid to rest on Prince Edward Island. The cemetery was beside the church he had attended as a little boy.

# All in Sport

# Football Game Won by Unconscious Player

It was November of 1923. The Texas Christian University freshman team was playing Terrell Prep. TCU beat Terrell by a score of 63–0. However, they would have lost if they had not had the help of an unconscious player.

TCU had only 20 players on its team. By the fourth quarter many of them had been injured. Finally, with only a couple of minutes left in the game, the coach looked around for a substitute. But there was no one left to send in!

TCU had only ten men on the field, but the rules say there must be eleven. The referees told the TCU coach that his team would forfeit the game unless they had the right number of players.

Just then, Ernest Lowry, who had been hurt on the opening kickoff, struggled up off a blanket and said, "I'm all right, coach. I'll go in." But the effort to sit up was too much for the boy and he passed out.

Suddenly, the frantic coach had an idea. He placed Lowry's blanket on the field just inbounds, and the unconscious boy was laid on it. He was far away from any action, but he was a legal eleventh man.

"We were on defense," the coach explained, "so Lowry could be any place back of the line of scrimmage. And he lay there during the final plays of the game. He gave us our eleventh man. It's the only time an unconscious player ever won a football game."

# Fair Trade

Istvan Gaal wasn't a great soccer player. He wasn't even average. He was terrible.

He was so bad he was traded to a rival team for a *soccer ball*!

Gaal was a 21-year-old Hungarian. In 1970, he moved to Canada. He bragged that he had been a star back in his native land. He had, he claimed, scored 31 goals in 44 games one season.

Everybody in the Canadian Soccer League wanted this promising young star. The Concordia Kickers signed him. And then they wondered what they had gotten.

"We didn't know what to make of him," said John Fisher, president of the Kickers. "He had a few moves, but he looked lousy. At first we thought he was holding back. He had just come to a new country and couldn't speak the language. We thought he'd be okay once he got used to everything. But he never improved."

Gaal wasn't on the starting team of the Kickers. He couldn't even make it as a substitute.

During a game, Fisher was talking with the owner of the

Toronto team. Recalled Fisher: "He said, 'The kid's bad, but maybe I can do something with him. Why don't you just release him to me?' I said, 'No, I'm not just going to *give* him to you. I want something out of the deal.' "

The Toronto owner smiled—and offered a soccer ball in exchange. Fisher quickly accepted.

"It was a good trade," said Fisher. "They got what they wanted, and I got a soccer ball. They go for $27.50, which is more than the guy was worth.

"The trade actually wasn't all that unusual," added Fisher. "I went checking through the records. I found that a hockey player was once traded for a pair of nets."

# Five on One

No basketball game has even been more unbelievable than that played in 1982 between Cal-Santa Cruz and West Coast Christian. In the game, five players took on a "team" of one—and lost!

Midway through the second half, West Coast was leading Santa Cruz by 15 points. Then they got into serious foul trouble. One after the other, West Coast players fouled out. Because of injuries, the team had only suited up eight players. When a fourth player was whistled out of the game, they could put only four men on the floor.

Still, West Coast held on to its lead.

But again and again the referee blew his whistle. Out went three more West Coast players. With 2:10 left to play, the team was down to one man: Mike Lockhart, a 6-foot, 1-inch guard.

According to the rules, a game can continue when a team has only one player left—if that team is leading.

When Lockhart found himself alone on the floor, West Coast was ahead 70–57. "I was really scared," he said. "I could dribble the ball, but there was nobody to pass to.

Also, I had four fouls myself, and one more and the game would be over. The worst part was inbounding the ball. The ref said I could only inbound it by having it touch a player on the other team."

Lockhart inbounded the ball by bouncing it off the leg of an opponent. Dribbling, weaving around all over the court, he ate up as much time as possible. Finally, he had to shoot. He missed, but managed to get his own rebound. Then he continued dribbling.

The Santa Cruz players couldn't believe what one man was doing to them. Frustrated, they kept grabbing at the ball, and fouled Lockhart—three separate times. Lockhart sank five of six free throws.

Almost every time Santa Cruz got the ball, they made a mistake. One player was called for traveling. Another missed an easy shot. Twice, in passing the ball, they threw it out of bounds.

Despite the fact they were playing five-on-one basketball, Santa Cruz scored only ten points. Lockhart scored five. The one-man basketball team held on to win, 75–67.

# Best Catch Ever

Tom Deal loved to play softball. A Saturday in the summer of 1981 found him playing the outfield for a local Chicago team. His team was ahead, and all they needed was one more out to win the game.

He watched as the pitcher streaked in a fastball. A solid *whap*, and a towering fly ball looped out toward Tom. It should have been an easy catch. But Tom flubbed it. The ball bounced off his glove.

The other team went on to score five runs and win the game. Tom felt sick. His team had lost, all because he had missed a very easy catch.

That night he fell asleep, still brooding about the ball he'd flubbed.

He awoke the next morning to the sound of a baby crying. Tom looked out the window of his apartment. Across the way was another apartment building. And out on a third-floor balcony was a months'-old baby. To Tom's horror, he could see that the baby was crawling toward the open railing of the balcony!

Tom threw on a robe and dashed downstairs and across

to the other apartment building. Frantic, he rang the door buzzer again and again. There was no answer. But high above he could still hear the crying baby.

He looked up. His heart stood still. The baby was *through* the railing! Then it was falling, plunging three stories—to its death.

There was no time to think, just to act. The baby tumbled head-over-heels down through the air. Arms outstretched, Tom dove. And made an impossible catch!

The toddler was unharmed.

For a long moment Tom sat on the pavement, holding the baby, hugging it. He grinned from ear-to-ear. Yesterday he had missed an easy catch, one that had lost a silly game. Now he had just made an unbelievable catch—and had saved a human life.

# Karate Team Knocks House Down

It was an interesting thing to watch. On a cold day in England not long ago, fifteen karate experts approached an old house. Then, using their hands, heads, and feet, they smashed the building to bits.

The six-room house was 150 years old and was due to be torn down anyway.

The team did not do the job just for fun. They did it to raise money for charity.

"It was a well-built house," said team leader Phil Milner. "It was a real challenge."

"The only hard part was the fireplace," said another member of the group. "It was made of about three tons of brick and cement."

The team, working in bare feet and karate suits, took six hours to destroy the place.

When it was all over, they bowed to the pile of rubble that had once been a house. Bowing to a defeated enemy is the final part of karate ceremony.

# His Own Worst Enemy

Henry Wallitsch is not well-known to boxing fans. He should be; he did something no other boxer has done in the history of the sport. In a match held in New York in 1959, he threw a wild and crazy punch—*and knocked himself out.*

When the bell rang starting the fight, Wallitsch was really ready. He was up against Bartolo Soni. Soni had beaten him six weeks earlier. Wallitsch wanted revenge.

He came out swinging. Not Soni. He kept hopping around and dancing away.

Wallitsch got hopping mad. He kept flailing away—and missing. Some of the fans in the crowd of 1,500 were laughing.

Finally, Wallitsch got Soni in a clinch. And now had come his big chance. As he broke free, Wallitsch wound up to deliver the punch of a lifetime. With all his strength, he threw a mighty haymaker at Soni.

And missed everything.

The force of the missed punch carried him across the ring—and right through the ropes. He fell headfirst, and took one right on the chin, from the arena floor.

Looking over the ropes, the ref counted out the unconscious Wallitsch. Then he raised Soni's right arm in a signal of victory.

Even though Soni never really landed a single punch, the record books show that he kayoed his opponent. But that's not quite fair. It's Wallitsch who threw the winning punch—even if it was himself he knocked out.

# Skier in Hot Water

Robert Rayor had been out for an afternoon of cross-country skiing through Colorado mountains. Suddenly, a snowbank gave way and he fell into an icy creek.

Rayor's wet clothes soon froze solid. He knew that if he tried to hike back to town he'd soon freeze to death.

Then an idea came to Rayor. He knew that not far away was a hot spring. It was his only hope.

Rayor hiked the short distance to the hot springs pool, took off all his clothes, and jumped in. The water was a comfortable 100 degrees.

For three days Rayor sat in the water, waiting to be rescued. Every so often he would drift off to sleep. But as soon as his head dropped underwater, he would immediately wake up.

Finally, Rayor was spotted by a rescue helicopter. The pilot dropped a backpack that contained food and clothing.

Rayor felt good. He assumed that the helicopter would be back shortly to rescue him. Then he noticed a note tied to a flare lying in the snow. Apparently, it had been knocked loose from the rest of the pack.

The note said that if he were Robert Rayor he should shoot off the flare. Since he hadn't done that, Rayor knew the helicopter would not return.

Rayor spent another night in the hot pool. The next morning he dried off as well as he could, put on the dry clothing the helicopter had dropped, and skied to a hospital.

All in all, Rayor was okay. Doctors found that he was suffering only from minor frostbite. They also found that he was very clean and his skin was wrinkled from the unusually long bath he had taken.

# Weird Weather

# Have You Ever Seen a Frozen Breath?

In Siberia, it is not uncommon to have temperatures of 50 degrees below zero. One day in 1901, however, the temperature plunged to 90 below!

People had to wear masks, or some sort of air-warming device, over their faces when they went outside. If they didn't, their breath would freeze in the air and fall to the ground! When the frozen breath hit the ground, it made a soft tinkling sound and shattered into tiny pieces.

Breathing out was fun to watch. But breathing in could kill. If a person were to inhale without a mask on, his or her lungs would be instantly coated with frost.

# Human Hailstones

It happened in 1930. Five men aboard a glider ran into bad weather. Their glider was lurching up and down. Ice coated the wings. Large hailstones were battering the craft to bits.

The five men decided to bail out. They checked their parachutes. Then one after the other, they jumped from the damaged craft.

For several seconds the men went into a free fall. They popped open their chutes. They continued their descent. All seemed to be going well.

Suddenly, a violent updraft lifted the men to the top of a cloud. There, they were coated with ice. Then they again began to fall. Down they drifted. Then another updraft caught hold of them. They soared skyward. They took on a second coating of ice, then again began to fall.

Over and over, the same thing happened. The men would descend. Then an air current would shoot them back up through the clouds. The coating of ice on their bodies became thicker and thicker.

The men may not have realized that they were going

through the same process that turns a raindrop into a hailstone. A raindrop loops up and down, gathering a layer of ice each time. When it is heavy enough, it falls.

Finally, the men were covered with ice. Each was a heavy ball of the stuff. In their parachutes, they dropped toward the earth. Like huge human hailstones, they swung back and forth on the ends of their lines.

When they hit the ground, the ice coating them shattered. All of them lay injured and in pain, and wondering at the amazing thing that had happened to them.

# A Little Heat Wave!

On July 6, 1949, a freak heat wave hit central Portugal. The temperature rocketed up to 158 degrees! Not only is this the highest temperature ever recorded in that country, it is the highest anywhere in the world.

The heat wave lasted for only two minutes. Moments later, the mercury shot down to 120 degrees.

Many scientists have studied this strange, short heat wave. So far, they've been unable to come up with a satisfactory explanation as to how or why it happened.

# Rain Out of a Clear Blue Sky

One day in 1958, Mrs. R. Babington returned home from an errand. She parked her car and started walking toward the back door of her house.

Suddenly it began to rain.

As she ran for cover, Mrs. Babington realized something was wrong. She stopped and looked up. Through the rain she could see the sun shining. There wasn't a single cloud in the sky!

At first Mrs. Babington thought a pipe had burst somewhere. Or perhaps the wind was picking up spray from a lawn sprinkler.

She began walking around her house, searching for the answer. But nowhere could she find a reason for the cloudless downpour.

When she walked out into the street, she realized the strangest thing of all. It was raining on her house, but nowhere else!

Soon, people began to gather in the street. They could see that rain was falling from the sky, but there were no clouds. And the rain was falling only in an area about 100 feet square.

For two and a half hours the water streamed down. Then, as suddenly as it had begun, the downpour stopped.

So far, no one has been able to explain the mystery. How is it possible for there to have been such a rain?